Have You Seen the Wind?

Kathleen Crawford
Illustrated by Jane Cope

A TAMARIND BOOK

Have You
Seen
the
Wind?

One night when everybody was tucked up in
bed, a strong wind began to blow.

     It whistled down the chimneys.

     It rattled letterboxes.

     It howled through the trees.

     In a little cottage, an old man and an
old woman were trying to sleep.

     The wind blew and blew.

Inside, the tabby cat was curled up in her basket. She heard the rattling and the whistling and the howling.

"It's too bad," she miaowed. "How can a cat sleep on a night like this?"

The next morning, the cat was very grumpy. "I know," she miaowed, "I'll go and find the wind and complain about all the trouble it has caused."

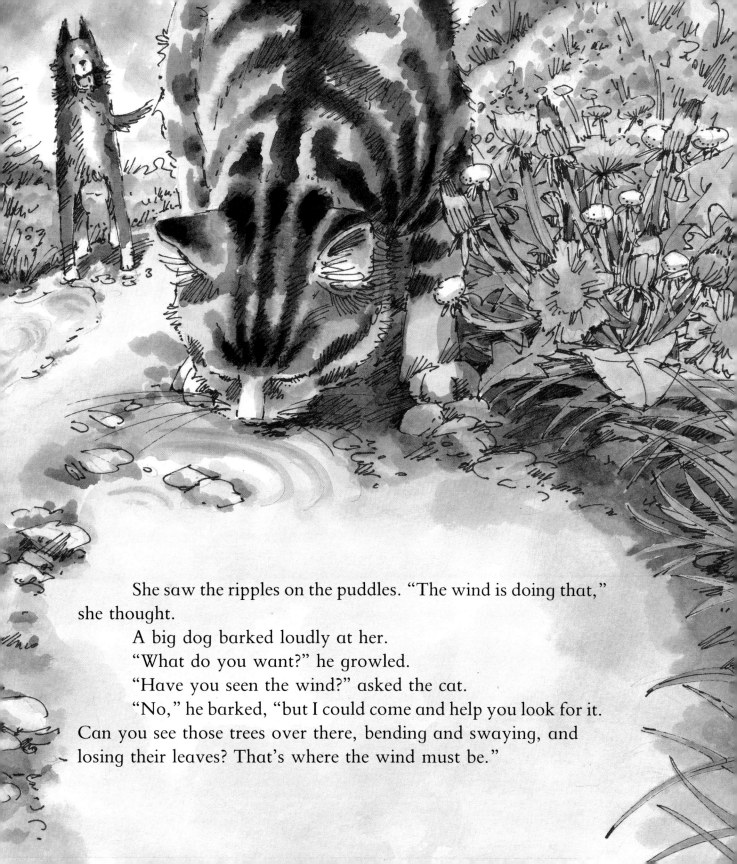

She saw the ripples on the puddles. "The wind is doing that,"
she thought.

A big dog barked loudly at her.

"What do you want?" he growled.

"Have you seen the wind?" asked the cat.

"No," he barked, "but I could come and help you look for it.
Can you see those trees over there, bending and swaying, and
losing their leaves? That's where the wind must be."

The cat and the dog walked down the lane until they reached the trees.

There was a carpet of leaves on the ground, and more were still falling. A squirrel was scurrying around looking for nuts for her winter store.

"Have you seen the wind?" they asked.

"No, I haven't," she said, "but I could come and help you look for it. Look over there on the hill. Some children are flying kites. That's where the wind must be."

So the cat and the dog and the squirrel
went on down the lane towards the hill.
Some sheep were grazing nearby.
"Have you seen the wind?" they asked
the sheep.

"No," bleated the sheep nearest to them,
"but I could come and help you look for it.
Look at the clouds moving across the sky. We
could try higher up the hill."

So the cat and the dog and the squirrel and the sheep climbed to the very top of the hill. Down in the valley they could see a lake. The boats were moving very quickly.

"Look how the sails are billowing," said the sheep. "That's where the wind must be, down there."

So they all ran down the hill as quickly
as they could until they came to the lake.
"Hello," they said to one of the ducks
swimming at the water's edge. "Have you
seen the wind?"

"I'm afraid not," he quacked, "but I could come and help you look for it. There's a field over there with a scarecrow in it. His hat's just blown away. Perhaps the wind is over there."

So the cat and the dog and the squirrel and the sheep and the duck went into the field. A few bright red poppies were swaying on their fragile stems, and some harvest mice were scampering about at the edge of the field.

"Have you seen the wind?" asked all the animals.

"No," squeaked the harvest mice, "but in that wood over there is an old oak tree. A wise old owl lives there and he knows everything. Would you like us to show you?"

"Yes, please," they replied wearily. They had walked a long way.

So the cat and the dog and the squirrel
and the sheep and the duck followed the
harvest mice into the middle of the wood.
High up in a gnarled old oak tree perched
the wise owl.

"Too-wit-too-woo," he hooted. "What
do you want? You're disturbing my sleep."

"Please," said the animals, "have you
seen the wind?"

"We've looked everywhere.
We saw it making ripples on the puddles,
making the trees sway,
blowing leaves on to the ground,
tossing kites into the air,
making the sails on the boats billow.
It even blew the scarecrow's hat on to
the hedge."

"And," said the tabby cat, "don't forget
all the noise it made in the night."

The old owl listened patiently.

"Listen," he said. "No one has ever seen the wind. You can hear the noise it makes, you can feel it blowing all around you, and you can see what it does to the trees, the kites and the boats. But you will never find out where it's going. Only God knows that. He knows where the wind comes from and where the wind is going. There are some things that only God understands."

The animals sighed. They were all very tired, especially the tabby cat who had walked the furthest. They thanked the wise old owl and started to walk home.

At last the tabby cat reached her cottage.

"Where have you been?" asked the old man and the old woman, giving her a saucer of creamy milk.

She lapped it up, purred and curled up in her basket by the warm fire where she soon fell fast asleep. She was just too tired to tell them.

A Tamarind Book
Published in association with SU Publishing
130 City Road, London EC1V 2NJ
ISBN 1 873824 14 9

First edition 1994

Printed and bound in Singapore